The wonder of the world,
The beauty and the power,
The shapes of things,
Their colours, lights, and shades—
These I saw.
Look ye also while life lasts.
—Anonymous

Henry Holt and Company, LLC • *Publishers since 1866*
175 Fifth Avenue, New York, New York 10010 • mackids.com

Henry Holt® is a registered trademark of Henry Holt and Company, LLC.
Copyright © 2013 by Benji Davies. All rights reserved.

Library of Congress Cataloging-in-Publication Data is available.

ISBN 978-0-8050-9967-6
First published in hardcover in 2013 by Simon & Schuster UK
First American edition—2014
Printed in China by Toppan Leefung Printing Ltd.,
Dongguan City, Guangdong Province.

10 9 8 7 6 5 4 3 2 1

THE STORM WHALE

Benji Davies

HENRY HOLT AND COMPANY
NEW YORK

Noi lived with his dad and six cats by the sea.

Every day, Noi's dad left early for a long day's work on his fishing boat.

He wouldn't be home again till dark.

One night, a great storm raged around their house.
In the morning, Noi went down to the beach
to see what had been left behind.

As he walked along the shore,
he spotted something in the distance.

As he got closer, Noi could not believe his eyes.

It was a little whale washed up on the sand.

Noi wondered what he should do.

He knew that it wasn't good for
a whale to be out of the water.

I must be quick! he thought.

Noi did everything he could to make the whale feel at home.

He told stories about life on the island.
The whale was an excellent listener.

The night was drawing in
and it was growing dark.

Noi was worried that his dad would be angry about having a whale in the tub.

Somehow Noi kept his secret
safe all evening.

He even managed to sneak some
supper for his whale.

But he knew it couldn't last.

Noi's dad wasn't angry.
He had been so busy, he hadn't noticed
that Noi was lonely.

But he said they must take the whale
back to the sea, where it belonged.

Noi knew it was the right thing to do,
but it was hard to say good-bye.

He was glad his dad was there with him.

Noi often thought about the storm whale.
He hoped that one day, soon . . .

. . . he would see his friend again.